MW01595689

WANDERING WINDS

A Collection of
20 Western Short Stories

by James J. Huble

Happy Birthday
Jerry

James J. Huble

GOOSE FLATS PUBLISHING   TOMBSTONE ~ ARIZONA

WANDERING WINDS
A Collection of 20 Western Short Stories
by James J. Huble

©2018 James J. Huble

ISBN# 978-1-939345-19-6

Library of Congress Control Number: 2018945281

First Printing June 2018

Published by
Goose Flats Publishing
P.O. Box 813
Tombstone, Arizona, 85638
www.gooseflats.com

All rights reserved. No portion of this book may be reproduced or transmitted in any form by any means, electronic or mechanical, including photocopying, recording, scanning to a computer disk, or by any information storage and retrieval system, without express permission in writing from the author and/or publisher. All characters appearing in this work are fictitious. Any resemblance to real persons, living or dead, is purely coincidental and unintentional.

DEDICATION

For my wife, Sandy,
and my sons, Ted and Pete

The winds wander across the plains
and through the canyons,
whispering their secrets
to those who will listen

James J. Huble

CONTENTS

THE MAJOR

The phantom moved stealthily through the Union Army camp. He cautiously made his way to the tent where General Grant was sleeping. He slipped inside. "Sergeant Price reporting from special scout," he bellowed.

General Grant, startled, sat up in bed and grumbled, "What the hell?" Grant picked up his timepiece from the table next to the bed, and examined it closely. "It's three o'clock in the morning, soldier. What in blazes are you doing in my tent?"

"Well, yes Sir, it's real early, sure enough. But that's the best and safest time to come through our pickets without getting shot. And I couldn't find no one else up an about, so I just come straight here to you."

Grant lit a lantern and called out for his orderly. "Find Colonel Henry and Major Morrison, and tell them to come here right away."

"While we wait for these gentlemen, tell me about this scouting report," said Grant.

"Yes Sir. You see, I was ordered to scout behind the Southern lines and learn as much as I could about numbers and locations and unit types. Major Morrison specifically told me to observe only. He cautioned me to make no contact." The sergeant chuckled. "I really like that bit about no contact. What did he think? I was going to take on the whole Confederate Army by myself?"

Grant coughed and tried to hide a chuckle of his own. "You're a cheeky little devil aren't you?"

"Yes Sir!" replied Price. "Specially about being a devil."

At this moment Colonel Henry and Major Morrison entered the tent.

Grant addressed the two officers. "This soldier has just returned from a scouting mission behind enemy lines. In addition to the information he is about to share, he has also demonstrated a severe breach in the security of the camp."

The two officers shuffled their feet, stared at one another, but made no reply.

"Can either of you explain how he was able to enter this camp and make his way to my tent without detection?" Grant paused waiting for some response. When none was forthcoming, he said, "This is a matter for us to discuss later. Sergeant, please make your report."

Sergeant Price then recited from memory the various Confederate installations he had seen. Of particular interest to General Grant was a supply depot. Stockpiled there were large quantities of wheat, corn, and beef. Also many small arms, rifles and pistols, being ready for distribution. And a barn full of black powder.

"That barn full of powder could be the Achilles heel." said Grant. "If one of our boys could sneak in there and blow that powder, it could destroy most or all of those supplies." He paused. "What do you think of that idea, Sergeant?"

"Sounds like a right smart plan, General. When are **you** going to sneak in there?

Grant started to laugh. "Yes, indeed, you are a most cheeky little devil. Besides me, who do you suggest?"

"How about Major Morrison," said Price smiling.

Grant contemplated quietly for sometime. Then at last he spoke. "This plan calls for absolute secrecy, and can best be carried out by two men in cooperation. As of now, only we four know, and I think it's best to keep things that way. Therefore, Sergeant, I'm going to accept your suggestion regarding Major Morrison. And you shall guide him."

So the plan was put into action. The next morning, just before dawn, the two men left the Union camp. Morrison started out at brisk pace walking upright like he was going for a hike in the woods. Price grabbed him, and shoved him down in the brush.

"Didn't they teach you nothin' in that academy you went to? You want to get shot by our own side before we even get started?"

"I didn't go to an academy, and don't you ever shove me again."

"How did you get to be an officer, then?"

"I bought my commission," said Morrison.

"God Almighty! It's bad enough I'm on a high risk mission. Now I find I'm saddled with a pampered popinjay. Well, let's get somthin' straight right now. You outrank me, but I'm the guide. I lead! You follow! And if I need to shove you in order to save your sorry ass, I will, Now keep your head down and try sneaking until I tell you it's ok to stand."

Major Morrison was appalled at being spoken to by an enlisted man in such a fashion. "When this is over, and we get back to camp, I intend to press insubordination charges."

"Major, I hope you do that, 'cause that'll mean we both got out of this mess alive."

The next few days the two moved slowly and cautiously toward their objective. They had a couple of close encounters with patrols in grey uniforms, but they managed to avoid detection.

Now they lay in the brush looking at the supply depot. The General's plan would work even better than expected because the powder barn was almost in the center of everything. That is, if they could blow it.

Each of the men carried a rifle and three pistols. And they had brought their own roll of blasting fuse so that they didn't have to search for that in the barn. They belly crawled to the end of the depot farthest away from the powder barn.

One of the men would slip unnoticed into the powder barn. This would require a great deal of patience, stealth, and luck. Once inside, he would connect the fuse to any of the powder kegs, and stretch it out long enough to allow some time to get away before the explosion. But not too long, that it might die out before touching off the powder. Since Price was the expert sneaker, and Morrison knew nothing about explosives, the choice was a no brainer.

This left Morrison with a very vulnerable task. He would lie in wait, keeping all the weapons except one pistol. He would watch Price, keeping track of him as much as possible. When Price was within a few yards of the powder barn, Morrison was to start shooting at anything and anyone other than the barn. This was to draw away any attention to what Price was doing. And by firing several weapons, it gave the illusion of a bigger force attacking. After firing most his rounds, Morrison was to run like hell into the brush and meet Price at an agreed place.

The diversion worked perfectly. Price was in and out of the powder barn in just a couple of minutes. Morrison sprinted away with bullets clipping the leaves around him. Then the barn exploded, and no one bothered about either man for a while. They met as planned.

Price knew they were not out of the woods yet. Undoubtedly a rebel patrol would be sent after them. They needed to move with speed, but also with caution. He kept a wary eye out for pursuit, but always kept moving. Morrison would stop and look back to see if they were followed. Price warned him to keep his head down, and just follow his lead, but Morrison still felt it was beneath his dignity to blindly take orders from an enlisted man. He stuck his head to see once more and took a rebel rifle ball in the eye.

Price quickly went back to the fallen officer. Dead! For Certain! Price stripped the coat from the body, and also took the spare pistol. It was always good to have an extra coat and gun.

Price got back to his camp in the middle of the afternoon. He much preferred coming in the dark, but he was tired and hungry. He saw a sentry, and called to him. "Who goes there?" came the challenge.

"I'm coming in from a scouting mission," answered Price.

"What's the password?"

"How the hell should I know? I been gone for a month."

"You stay where you are until I can get my sergeant."

When the sentry returned with the sergeant, they brought two more soldiers with them. Price didn't recognize any of these men. "Whoever you are, stand up and move forward very slowly. Keep your hands where we can see them." Price did as he was told. Then the sergeant exclaimed, "Aw, gee, Major. I didn't know ya was an officer." Price hesitated for just a couple of seconds and then realized he was wearing Morrison's coat.

As Price was paraded through the camp he could see that this was a completely different outfit than the one he had left. He didn't see anyone that he knew or knew him.

"Well, Major. You look like you've been through somewhat of an ordeal. I'm Colonel Warren. My men and I have only been in this camp for a week. If you were attached to the Army that left here, I'm afraid you won't catch them now. I have no idea where they might have gone."

They kept addressing him as Major. He wondered just how long he could keep up such a charade. Dare he even try? Maybe he should tell them the truth. The coat was that of a dead officer, and he borrowed it to stay warm and dry.

"What's your name, Major?" The moment was upon him. Aw, what the hell, he thought. "Morrison, Sir." Now why did he pick that name? Well, this whole crazy situation was one big farcical gamble. If they checked, there was a Major Morrison. And he wasn't going to tell.

"Major Morrison, welcome. I heard that you said you have just returned from a scout mission. Was it successful?"

"Yes, Sir. Very!"

"Like to brag a little, maybe?" the Colonel asked smiling.

"No, Sir. Just stating a fact."

"Well, it so happens that I am in need of a good chief of scouts. Since you are at liberty, so to speak, I suggest that you assume that position."

Major Morrison performed his duties as chief of scouts with exemplary efficiency. He received numerous accolades and won many medals during the next year of the war. It was this fame that brought him to a special gathering of officers and civilian officials.

"Major Morrison," said Colonel Warren taking him by the arm. "Allow me to introduce you to General Grant." Morrison froze.

"Come now Major, you needn't falter. General Grant is gracious and easy going."

Leading the Major to Grant's side, the Colonel said, "General, this is the Major Morrison you've been hearing about."

General Grant turned and extended his hand, and then starred at Major Morrison. "I believe we've met once before, am I not right?"

Major Morrison cleared his throat, twisted his head as if shaking off some pain in his neck, and replied, "That we have...Sir."

Grant smiled. "Are you still a cheeky little devil?"

Morrison gulped. "Yes, Sir. Specially about being a devil."

"Well, we need good officers wherever and however we get them." Grant turned left the room. ♣

LAW OF NATURE

Angus McPherson reined his big bay gelding to a halt in front of the small frame house, and fired two shots into the air. He, and the three hired hands riding with him, watched as the door to the house opened slowly. The homesteader, Jonathon Adams, peered out carefully.

McPherson owned the largest spread in the county, and he ran roughshod over any and all other persons who dared to settle in what he called "his valley". He was the big wheel, even though in stature he was only five foot five, and weighed 145 pounds. A remarkably ugly face matched his surly disposition. He controlled by force with the help of hired guns. McPherson had ordered several homesteaders to move, and most of them had. But Adams was a stubborn hold-out.

"Yer clearin' out ta day, Adams," shouted McPherson. "I'm givin' ya 'til noon ta pack up and hit the trail. If yer still here when me and the boys come back, we aim ta shoot holes in yer building ta drive ya out." With that McPherson and his three hired gunmen rode away.

Adams stood in the yard watching them. He was joined by his wife Sarah. "Dammit," he stammered. "It ain't right. We got a legal claim ta this land. We ain't givin' it up!"

"Mister McPherson already owns so much land. What is so important about ours?" asked Sarah. "He won't really come back and shoot us. No one can be that mean hearted."

"Well, if he does come back, you make sure you and the kids are in the back room. I'll try and talk some sense to him from the front door."

Shortly after noon McPherson returned with his three hired gunmen. As they were dismounting Adams started to step through his front door. He was met with a hail of gunfire.

With bullets striking the door, splintering the frame and sill, Adams dove back into the house, and managed to kick the door closed without being hit.

For the next few minutes the house was peppered with bullets. The glass in the front window exploded, and the window frame was shattered. The door looked like a sieve.

The shooting stopped and McPherson shouted, "I warned ya what would happen if ya didn't leave. I gave ya time ta load up yer things in yer wagon and be gone. Now times run out. Ya hear me, Adams? I'll still let ya git in yer wagon and go right now. But you'll just hafta fergit packin' up things. Yer stuff can burn just like yer house."

The front door opened and Sarah Adams stepped out. She wore a faded cotton dress that was covered in front with a well worn apron. She brushed hair away from her grim face, and her eyes blazed with anger.

Walking directly toward the four men, Sarah stopped about five feet in front of McPherson. She glared at the men and said, "You must be real proud of yourselves, shooting at a woman and kids. Yes, kids.

My little boy and girl are in there. You might have killed them."

Sarah spit at McPherson. "You are a dirty, contemptible, greedy swine. I hope you rot in hell." Her right hand slid beneath the apron, and grasped the Colt that was hanging from a leather thong tied to her waist. She fired through the apron. Six slugs slammed into McPherson.

Sarah spoke with grave composure. "You should never threaten a mama bear's cubs." ♣

HE NOT SAY

Bull Avery and Shorty Dennison followed a narrow mountain trail to where it passed between two huge boulders. Stepping out of the rocks they entered a clearing and saw an old Mexican dressed in a tattered serape and a battered sombrero.

"Buenos dias," Mexican as he turned a stick with meat on it over a fire that was surrounded by a ring of stones. "You eat de cascabel?" he asked smiling.

Bull and Shorty just starred at him agape.

"Rattlesnake," said the Mexican gesturing with the stick. "Es muy bien!"

"Don't recall as I ever et rattlesnake." said Shorty. "You, Bull?"

"No. Me neither," replied Bull.

"You want?" asked the Mexican.

Bull looked at Shorty, who shook his head. "We'll pass," he answered.

The Mexican grinned and popped a piece of meat into his mouth.

"Ya got anythin' ta drink?" asked Bull.

"Agua," replied the Mexican.

"What about whiskey?" asked Shorty. "Ya got any whiskey?"

"Estoy apendado. Only water," said the Mexican. As he reached for the water a small deerskin bag fell from his pocket. Shorty was quick to pick it up.

"Well, what do we have here?" he drawled. Opening the bag, he poured some gold dust into his hand. Showing Bull he said, "Look at this."

Bull stepped over to the Mexican and asked, "What's yer name?"

"Manuel."

"So, Manuel, you found some gold."

"Si, Senor."

" Do you remember where you found this gold?"

"Si, Senor. I know what trail I followed to where I find the gold."

"Could you find that trail again?"

"Si, Senor."

"OK, Manuel. You're gonna take us to this trail," said Bull.

Manuel stood, and kicked dirt on to the fire. He smiled and nodded, walking over to the two huge boulders. He gestured for Bull and Shorty to follow.

The three men descended the trail that Bull and Shorty had followed to the clearing. At the bottom, Manuel led them along the base of the mountain until they came to another trail. "This is trail I followed," said Manuel.

"That's good, Manuel. Now lead the way," said Bull. "We'll see if you been tellin' the truth."

Manuel nodded and started up the trail. It twisted and turned and finally the three men entered a clearing.

"What the hell?" shouted Bull. "This is the same clearing we found you in."

"Si, Senor. Is the same. I follow different trail than you."

"This is where ya found the gold?" bellowed Shorty.

"Si, Senor," said Manuel smiling.

"Why didn't ya say this before?"

"You not ask where I find gold. I answer questions you asked."

"Why you worthless greaser," screamed Shorty. "I ought ta plug ya just fer bein' so damn simple minded."

"Now, Shorty," interrupted Bull. "Ain't no call ta be shootin' him. 'Sides he ain't told us exactly where he found the gold." Bull stepped close to Manuel and glared. "So, where did you find the gold?"

"Right over here," said Manuel walking to a cluster of rocks piled up on one another.

"That looks like a grave," said Shorty.

"Si, I bury him," said Manuel.

"You buried who?" asked Bull.

"The man who had the gold," answered Manuel.

"You killed him?" exclaimed Shorty.

"No, Senor. I only bury him. Find bag of gold when I put him in grave."

"So, where did this gold dust come from?" shouted Bull.

Manuel shrugged and grinned. "He not say. He dead." ♣

HORSE THIEF

Mark Trent pulled up his sorrel in front of the corral at the Circle CW. He dismounted, wrapped the reins around a post, and started off to find Frank Greer, the ranch foreman. He found Frank in the hay barn along with Curt Wright, owner of the Circle CW. Trent removed his hat in deference to the owner's presence.

"What's up, Mark?" asked Greer.

"I just come in from the South pasture," said Trent. "There's another mare missing."

"Damn!" cursed Greer. "That makes five in the last month, Mr. Wright."

"Seems we got us a horse thief, Boys," replied Wright. "Ben Tillson said he's lost a few mares, and Clark Ames had a couple stole."

"We ain't had any trouble with rustlers fer several years," said Greer. "And why horses? If it was cows one at a time like this, I'd guess they was bein' butchered. But horses?"

"Well, whoever it is," answered Wright, He's being mighty careful by taking only one at a time, and from different ranches. Probably plans to build a herd, and then sell 'em somewhere."

"Maybe he's already got a buyer," said Trent. "If so, he won't need ta keep 'em long."

"You hear of anyone buyin' horses lately?" asked Wright.

Both Trent and Greer shook their heads, and said "No."

A couple of nights later, a meeting of the ranchers and their foremen was arranged to discuss the horse thief problem. Nobody knew of anyone buying horses. No one had seen or heard of any strangers who might be suspects.

"The damn cheeky devil!" sputtered Jake Simms. "Last night he come right into the ranch yard, and took a mare I had in a special corral. I was gonna take her down to Phillipe Herrera's and breed her to one of his Arabians." Various astonished comments responded.

"One very interesting thing," continued Simms. "The horse he was ridin' was unshod."

"What about boot prints?" someone asked.

"None. He never dismounted," replied Simms. "Lifted the gate latch and drove the mare out. Left the gate open."

"That sounds like a Indian trick," said Hank Pierce, one of the foremen.

"We ain't had any trouble from Indians since they moved onto the reservation," said Ben Tillson.

"Just the same, we should probably take a look around that Indian camp.

"Yeah, and we should also look around the Jessup place. His kid rides an unshod pony," remarked Clark Ames.

Curt Wright spoke up. "It won't hurt to take a look in both places. But we got to go easy. We can't accuse somebody of horse stealing just because they own an unshod horse."

A check of the reservation turned up nothing. John Dennis, the agent, was sure that none of his Indians had been off the reservation.

Pony Stealer laughed. "I can do this and he not know. But I not steal. Look in camp. Maybe we hide horses in tepees." He laughed again.

The Jessup boy was terrified, when they questioned him. He had heard that they hang horse thieves. His father was indignant and very angry. "You should be ashamed of scarring my kid. He's too young ta know how ta steal a horse."

"Well, maybe it was you ridin' the kid's horse," snarled one of the men.

"If it was me, ya think I'd be dumb enough ta keep 'em here?"

Curt Wright edged his bay forward. "I'm sorry, Mr. Jessup. The boys got a little carried away. We won't bother you again. If you should hear anything about our missing mares would you please let me know."

The horse stealing tapered off. None of the ranchers had lost any animals in the last three weeks. Mark Trent dismounted and headed across the ranch yard to where Frank Greer and Curt Wright were talking. Trent had a big grin on his face.

"I saw that horse thief this afternoon," he said cheerfully.

Greer and Wright turned to look at Trent.

"He's a big, mean lookin' fella with a scar on his face. He had about twenty five mares with him over by Sweetwater Canyon. I only saw him for a couple of minutes before he disappeared into an arroyo. He's damn smart. He'll be nigh onto impossible ta catch."

"You're sure he's the horse thief?" asked Wright.

"You bet. I recognized some of the mares. And he truly is a....horse....thief. He's a big chocolate colored mustang stallion." Trent stood there still grinning like a little kid. ♣

GUNMAN'S SUNSET

Tucson, Arizona, 1898. Two old gunfighters, Aaron Tate and Palmer Fariday, were sitting in the dining room of the Occidental Hotel.

"You ride in from Santa Fe?" asked Tate.

"Yes, but not on horseback," replied Fariday. "I don't cotton much ta ridin' horses anymore. Too many aches and pains. I come in on the Atchison, Topeka."

"Know whatcha mean," said Tate. "Rode in on the Southern Pacific myself. Lot more comfortable than forkin' a bronc."

"Heard you was a lawman in Yuma," said Fariday.

"Was for a spell. Mostly lockin' up drunks. Then the town fathers decided a fifty year old gunslinger wasn't the right man for the job."

"What made 'em decide that?"

"Oh, some young punk thought he'd raise a little hell by shootin' up the Palace Saloon.

I didn't wade right in and brace him. Didn't feel it was necessary ta kill the kid, and also didn't figure ta take a bullet foolishly. The saloon owner, who happen ta be the mayor, didn't see it that way."

"That's the trouble with havin' a gunman's reputation. There's always someone who thinks you should always charge in with guns blazin', or else some squirt who thinks he's faster 'n better than you, and is out ta prove it," grumbled Fariday. "I'm fifty two myself, and all I got is several scars and a reputation."

"It ain't dyin' that bothers me so much," said Tate. "And when I took up the gun, I never figured on dyin' in bed." Fariday smiled and nodded. "But," continued Tate, "I don't figure on throwin' my life away for some cause I don't believe in. And I sure as hell don't intend to let some punk make his reputation by killin' me."

"Damn!" exclaimed Fariday. "That's sure enough how I feel. But I'm getting' tired a pullin' my gun."

The two men sat in silence for a couple of minutes. Then as if of one mind, they both rose and left the hotel. They walked side by side without speaking to the Hand and Foster Saloon.

The gunmen sat starring at each other while sipping their beer. Then Fariday said, "Last month in Las Cruces some loud mouthed punk called me out. The little shit wasn't even eighteen, but he was out to make a reputation. Oh, he was fast as a rattler, but the dumb ass couldn't shoot worth a damn. His first shot missed me completely. The second barely grazed my ribs. I didn't want ta kill him. But I wasn't gonna let him gloat over my dead body."

Tate smiled and nodded. "Choosin' a time ta die is somethin' we've earned," he said.

The two gunmen sipped their beer in silence. Then once again they rose as one and left the saloon.

Tate and Fariday walked together to the park on the edge of Tucson. They stepped up onto the raised open stage that was there. They faced each other about twenty paces apart, and smiled and nodded.

The two gunmen's hands moved in unison to their revolvers. Not fast. Deliberate. They weren't trying to beat each other. It wasn't a duel. It was a noble ritual. The guns cleared leather smoothly from many years of practice. They came up level and steady. Matching holes appeared in the shirt pocket of each man.

It was sunset in Tucson, Arizona. ♣

NUGGETS

aleb Purdy picked his way slowly and carefully through the maze of rocks as he descended the rugged mountain trail. He carried a stick about six feet in length, and used it sometimes for balance and sometimes to probe the rocks for rattlesnakes. Twice he had almost stepped on a rattler. That could be a deadly mistake.

Caleb had been searching for gold in these mountains for a couple of months, but so far had found nothing. Tired, hungry and thirsty he decided to give up. At least for a little while. He would rest for a time back at his cabin, where his daughter, Edna, was waiting. He looked forward to eating her fine meals. And she would wash and mend his dirty, trail dusty clothes while he rested.

Edna was twenty years old. A fine house-keeper, and a good cook. But unfortunately, she was worse than plain looking, and thus had no callers. This, of course, was very advantageous to Caleb.

As Caleb rounded a bend in the rocky, twisted trail he halted abruptly. Standing there were two heavily laden pack mules. And on the ground beside them lay a man.

Caleb moved cautiously toward the trio. He didn't want to spook the mules as he looked over the situation. He knelt beside the man, an old prospector by appearances. The man was dead. Upon examination Caleb could see where the man had been snake bit. The image of his own close encounters made him shudder.

Caleb stood. Speaking softly to the mules, he approached them slowly. He carefully partially opened one of the packs. His jaw dropped as he gazed dumb struck at the contents. Gold ore! Rich gold ore! The old prospector had made a strike. Caleb looked down at he man's body. Poor old devil. What a time to die.

The ground was much too hard and rocky to dig a proper grave. However, Caleb felt duty bound to bury the body of his unexpected benefactor. Finding a crevice, he pushed the body inside and covered it with rock.

Caleb never told anyone, not even Edna, how he came by the gold ore. At regular intervals, he converted the ore into cash at the assay office a little at a time. People assumed he had a vein somewhere that he visited as needed. He helped sustain this myth by going off into the mountains at various times. Some men tried to follow him to his secret place. But, of course, no one ever saw it, since it didn't exist.

Three years later Caleb died. Edna, still an uncourted spinster, was now making the trips to the assay office with gold ore. Now men began to take an interest. She was not going off into the mountains, so the gold ore must be stashed. And she knew where.

Frank Stillwell was already a prosperous land owner in the community. But he was greedy.

Although he had several mistresses over the years, he had never married. Why buy a cow, when milk is cheap? However, Edna's gold ore was tantalizing. Frank began a fervent courtship, and Edna was swept off her feet.

Of course, Frank wasn't really serious about marrying Edna. But he had to make it look good if he wanted to find that gold ore. He had a plan. A deceitful plan.

Frank met with a stranger passing through the area. He paid the stranger to pose as a minister for the purpose of performing the wedding ceremony between he and Edna. He even purchased a marriage license, which he showed to Edna.

As soon as the ceremony was over, Frank asked Edna to show him where the gold ore was hidden. Edna agreed, but said that first she would move into Frank's beautiful, grand mansion. After all, she was his wife now.

One week later, Edna, having made herself very comfortable in Frank's spacious palatial manor, told Frank where he could find the gold. When Frank returned, he was furious. He had found the gold ore packs, but they were now nearly empty. He ordered Edna out of the house.

"But this is my home now," said Edna very sweetly. "I am your wife."

"Don't be ridiculous!" shouted Frank. "Do you think I would really marry a hag like you?"

"The minister was a phony I hired, so we're not married! I'll bring him here to prove it!" Frank whirled and stormed out of the house. A few minutes later, he returned with the stranger in tow.

"Tell this stupid cow," yelled Frank, "that you are not a minister, and that she and I are not man and wife!"

The stranger meekly stammered, "I am not a minister."

"There, you see!" screamed Frank.

"However," continued the stranger, "it seemed most charming that the groom wanted me to pose as a minister to keep his bride happy, when he didn't really want a church wedding. So I agreed. I assumed my position as the new Circuit Judge for this area was known. You are in fact man and wife." ♣

CUT THE DECK

It was a lazy, early Tuesday evening in the Red Garter Saloon. Bart Simpson was behind the bar polishing glasses, preparing for the usual nightly crowd. Taking advantage of the lull in the towns activity, Sheriff Morgan Stark sat at a table sipping his beer, watching the card game at the table across the room.

Five men, two circle-x cowhands, the town barber, the hotel clerk, and a stranger, were playing poker. Stark studied the stranger as he skillfully shuffled and dealt the cards. No doubt a professional gambler and the pile of money in front of him certainly supported this assumption.

The professional was good. Very clever. The other men at the table each won a small pot once in a while. The bigger pots always went to the gambler.

Suddenly one of the cowhands kicked back his chair violently, and jumped up. "You're cheating, you lousy card sharp!"

The gambler looked up at the cowhand and softly said, "I'm sorry you feel that way, Son. It is unfortunate that you are a bad poker player. It is even a greater misfortune that you are a poor loser."

The cowboy started to reach for his gun when he heard Sheriff Stark's warning. "Don't touch your gun, Billings. I wouldn't want to have to shoot you." The sheriff had risen quickly when the cowboy kicked back his chair, and was now standing directly in back of him. Stark reached over and removed the gun from Billings' holster. "Just in case," he said. Crossing to the bar he placed the gun on top.

Returning to the poker table the sheriff addressed the stranger. "What's your name?" The gambler, still seated, replied, "Hap Cole."

"I've been watching you, Mister Cole. It's obvious that you are a highly skilled professional. You could be cheating as Mister Billings has accused."

"Yes, I could," replied Cole. "But I didn't. I don't have to cheat to beat these amateurs."

"Why you lying skunk," hollered Billings as he lunged toward the table. "Billings!" bellowed the sheriff. The cowboy stepped back.

Stark picked up the deck of cards and examined them. He didn't notice anything unusual. He spread them out on the table, and then restacked them.

"You, Mister Cole, are a gambler by profession. And you, Mister Billings, are by choice a gambler today." Stark paused, and starred at the two men. He tapped the deck and said, "Let the cards determine a resolution."

The sheriff spread the cards out on the table face down. "Gentlemen, you may each draw a card from the deck. Mister, Cole, if you draw the higher card, we will presume that you are not cheating, and the money is yours."

Billings' hand moved hesitantly over the deck, and then selected a card. He looked at the card and then slapped it face up on the table. A queen. Cole casually picked a card and turned it over. A nine.

"You lost, skunk. The money's mine!" shouted Billings triumphantly.

"Wait just a moment, Billings," said Stark. "That's not exactly what I stated. I proposed if Cole won the draw it would be evidence he was not cheating, and the money would be his. I did not say if he lost you would get the money."

"What the hell are you trying to pull?" snarled Billings.

"Well, the card draw was a test," replied Stark. "All Cole had to do to establish his innocence and keep the money was to win the draw. But he didn't win." Stark paused. That means either he hasn't been cheating, or he was clever not to win."

Billings looked at the sheriff and sputtered, "So what did you prove?"

"Well, I didn't prove anything. But I did raise a question of reasonable doubt. So I'm acting as judge and jury in this case." Both Billings and Cole starred at Stark with surprised and confused looks.

"How much money do you have in the pot, Billings?"

"Eighty-five dollars."

"Do you agree with that, Mister Cole?"

"I believe that to be correct."

"Mister Billings, take eighty-five dollars. I don't want to see you playing poker in here again."

"Mister Cole, the rest of the money is yours. If I have any reason in the future to believe you are cheating, I'll let you sit in my jail for a couple of weeks and then run you out of town. There will be no chance of a reprieve by the draw of cards. I already drew and you lost." ♣

THE TRAMP

The old tramp rode into Beaver Creek on a swayback horse that was so skinny it looked like it might collapse in the middle of the street at any moment. The man riding the crow-bait was a perfect match for the animal. Rail thin all skin and bones. Long disheveled hair sticking out from under weather beaten hat. A scrawny beard. He probably hadn't shaved in some time, but he was one of those men who just couldn't grow a decent beard. His clothes were wrinkled and dirty, but they were not torn or patched.

The horse moved at an ambling gate. The rider drew up in front of the livery stable, and dismounted. He rolled from the saddle in a way that almost appeared he had fallen off.

Ben Emory stepped out from the stable. He scornfully appraised both the horse and the tramp. "You figure to put that bag-a-bones in my stable?"

The tramp smiled and patted the horse's neck. "You got any money?" asked Emory. The tramp continued smiling. "Just what I thought, a deadbeat." snarled Emory. "I suppose you figured on sleeping with your horse." The tramp hung his head and peered up sheepishly. "Get outta here. I ain't runnin' no house a charity."

"I could muck out the stable," said the tramp quietly. "I said git!" retorted Emory.

The tramp turned away and led his horse to the edge of town. He picketed the animal, not worried about someone stealing it. Then he walked slowly back into town.

It was Saturday, and Beaver Creek was very busy. The tramp made his way to the Silver Nugget Saloon, pushed through the double

swinging doors, and moseyed about among the crowd. He was hoping someone might offer to buy him a drink. He was jostled about several times, occasionally very rudely. Once he was actually knocked down. No one seemed to notice him on the floor. No one helped him get up.

He stood by the bar for a short time. The bartender asked "What'l it be?" The tramp smiled and shrugged. "Looking for a handout are ya, old bum?" scowled the barman. "I ain't got time fer the likes a you. I got paying folks ta serve." With that the barman walked away to the other end of the bar. The tramp looked about the room, and then quietly left the saloon.

As the tramp walked down the main street of Beaver Creek he passed the mercantile just as a lady emerged from the store juggling several packages. "Let me help you with those," he said politely. The lady lurched away from him and screamed, "Stay away from me you filthy creature. Don't you dare touch my things!" Disgustedly she turned, and hurried away in a huff almost dropping one of her packages.

The tramp found his way to a small park. There he sat down on a bench overlooking the creek for which the town was named. A young woman glanced at him as she walked by. She stopped and looked back. Then she returned to the bench and sat beside him.

"Are you hungry?" asked the young woman. The tramp nodded. "Do you have any money?" The tramp shook his head. "When was the last time you had something to eat?" The tramp shrugged. "You poor man," said the young woman. "I'm the waitress at the Bread and Butter Café." She reached over and took his hand. "Come with me," she said.

They entered the café, and the tramp was seated at one of the tables. There were several other customers. They all stared at the tramp with contempt. A couple of them immediately left before finishing their meals. The young woman set a plate of hot food on the table for the tramp. He looked at her, and smiling said quietly "Thank you very much. You are a saint."

The man who owned the café came into the dining room. One the other patrons motioned to him. As they spoke gestures were made toward the tramp. The young woman was standing by the tramp's table when the owner approached. Addressing his comments to the young lady he said, "My other customers are offended by this man's presence. Please escort him from the premises, and do not bring him in again!"

The young woman starred at her employer. Then she looked at the tramp and said, "I'm so very sorry." He smiled at her and replied, "That's alright, my dear. I understand."

The rest of Saturday was similar. The tramp was rebuffed and scorned wherever he went. He returned to the park bench, and was sitting there late in the evening when the young woman came to his side again. "I'm really sorry about what happened at the café today." The tramp smiled at her. "I thought you would probably be sleeping out by your horse, so I brought you a blanket." The tramp smiled again and said, "Thank you. You truly are a saint."

The next day was Sunday, so the residents of Beaver Creek were gathered at the church. The tramp entered the place of worship, and heard a collective sigh of scorn. No one moved to make a place for him. A couple of men actually stood with folded arms barring him from seating.

He ended up in front of the pulpit where the preacher was standing. The minister looked down upon him. Even he seemed to view the tramp as a leper. "Since this is a house of God, I cannot actually turn you out. But as you can clearly see you are not welcome here. Therefore, on behalf of my congregation, I ask you to please leave." The tramp smiled and left the church. He walked to the edge ot town, mounted his horse and rode away.

On the Sunday one week later a handsome carriage drawn by a beautiful matched pair of horses drove down the main street of Beaver Creek and stopped in front of the church. A polished,

well groomed man wearing very expensive clothes exited the carriage and entered the church. To the amazement of the congregation, it was the same man who had appeared before them a week earlier as a tramp. Again he made his way to the front. He then turned to address them.

"On my previous visit to your community I found almost all of you to be rude, selfish and uncharitable. You hold yourselves in such high regard, it's a wonder that you even talk to **each other**."

He paused for a moment. "One exception!" He moved down the aisle and stopped. He gestured to the young woman who had been kind to the tramp. "Please come forward, my saint." The young woman shyly stepped into the aisle. "Please accept this check for ten thousand dollars in gratitude for kindness to an old tramp. I suggest that you deposit it in the bank as soon as possible, lest these vultures try to snatch it away. Again I thank you. You are my saint." ♣

MEDICINE WAGON

Two hours after leaving San Luis, Colorado, a wagon wheel fell off. Nothing was broken. The wheel pin had been jarred loose by the wagon bouncing over the rock strewn terrain. The young lad, really not much more than a boy, had walked along the way he had come, and found the pin about a half mile back.

Now he stood beside the wagon, staring at the wheel on the ground. Although he was a strong lad, big for his age, with well muscled arms, there was no way he could manage to lift the wagon and replace the wheel by himself.

It was a medicine show wagon, fully equipped with the supplies of this trade. The wagon belonged to the lad's uncle, Professor J. T. Masterson. Masterson's amazing all purpose tonic and cure all oil, at two dollars a bottle, was the source of income. It was also the reason the lad was alone on the trail.

The lad's uncle, who's name was really Axel Harris, had been exposed as a charlatan, and lynched by an angry mob of customers in San

Luis. It was only the lad's young age that saved him from a similar fate. He was, however, ordered out of town, and told never to return.

So he left San Luis, and was now traveling north. He had been told to follow the Sangre de Cristo mountains on the east, and this would take him to Fort Garland.

As he stood staring at the fallen wheel, he was startled by a cackling voice behind him. "Howdy."

The young lad spun around and saw an old man leading a pack mule. The old man spit. "Good thing I'm a friendly cuss."

The lad just gawked speechless.

"You dumb as well as deaf?" cackled the old man. "Me n' Jenny made enough noise comin' up on ya."

The lad stammered, "Na...No, I ain't deaf ner dumb. I was just thinkin' hard 'bout this wheel and not payin' attention to nothin' else."

"Not payin' 'tention is a might good way ta git yer hair lifted, youngin."

The lad didn't reply. The old man looked down at the fallen wheel, and spit again. "Don't look broke," he said.

"It ain't. But I can't get it back on the wagon by myself."

"Too bad. Looks like a nice wagon. You got any whiskey?"

The lad shook his head.

"You this professor fella?"

"No, that's my uncle. Err...that was my uncle. He's...ah...dead."

"So, what's this snake oil yer peddlin'?"

"Ain't me doin' that," sputtered the lad. I just played the banjo and sang to attract all the people."

"Ya got any now?"

"I don't know. Maybe."

"Well, how 'bout I jess look in these here boxes," cackled the old man. "Now, lookee here," he said holding up a bottle. "Since you ain't sellin' this stuff, I reckon you won't mind iffin I take a little nip."

The old man uncorked the bottle and gulped down a big swig. His face turned red, his eyes got glassy, and he shook his head several times. "Whoeee! What in tarnation is this stuff?"

"I don't know. It's somethin' my uncle stirred up."

"Damnation," gasped the old man. "I polished off some mighty mean panther piss in my day, but this stuff is pure poison."

"Maybe that's why they hanged my uncle back in San Luis."

The old man spit again. "They hanged him? Fer real?"

The lad nodded.

"Damnation," hollered the old man. Then he tipped the bottle into his mouth and gulped 'til it was empty. He smacked his lips, wiped his hand across his face, and sat down on the ground. He was sitting there dazed when the Kiowas appeared.

Six Kiowa braves on spotted ponies. They each carried a lance, no guns or bows.

The old man tried to stand, but under the influence of Professor Masterson's cure all, he tumbled. The young lad stood frozen with fear.

As the warriors moved their ponies slowly toward the medicine wagon, they carried their lances upright. The old man mumbled something about scalps tied to the lances. The Kiowas jabbered among themselves. They seemed to be curious about the wagon with its colorful pictures and lettering, and the many things hanging from hooks.

One of the warriors leaped from his pony, and walked boldly to the wagon, ignoring the two white men. His gaze went directly to the shiny banjo, silver body with pearl inlaid neck.

He reached up to remove the banjo from its hook, and almost dropped it, because it was heavier than he expected. The young lad instinctively caught the instrument, and held it steady with the brave. Then the lad's finger strummed the strings a couple of times.

The Kiowa called to his companions, and they dismounted and walked to the wagon. They looked at the banjo, and two of them plucked at the strings. Then the first brave thrust the banjo into the lad's hands, and grunted. The lad understood, and started to play and sing.

The old man couldn't believe his eyes. That snake oil he drank mustta really ratttled his brain. The lad was playing and singing, and the Kiowas were trying to sing along.

The Indians then began to fumble through some costumes that were hanging on the wagon. When they found some wigs, they became very excited. They waved the wigs around in the air, and nodded to the lad. Then one of the braves dangled a golden haired wig in front of the lad, and made some guteral sounds. Then he shook his lance and gestured to the scalps hanging there.

By now the old man was sobering up some, and could speak enough Kiowa to figure out what was going on. He spoke quietly to the lad. "That brave wants ta trade scalps with ya. He wants ta have that golden one fer his lance."

"But that ain't no scalp," sputtered the lad. "That's a wig."

"Well, he don't see it that way, n you best don't be tellin' him no different. N you better show you like the scalp he gives ya."

So the trade was made. The Kiowas then helped put the wheel back on the wagon.

Before the Kiowas rode away, the old man gave them each a bottle of Professor Masterson's tonic, but told them, "No drink now...go home... drink!" ♣

MEXICAN COWS

For the last few day Gil Tripp and Mike Barr had been chousing mavericks out of the dense brush along the Rio Grande. The work was hot, dusty, tiring, and sometimes dangerous, but they were young, strong men who thrived on excitement.

They had managed to gather just over thirty cows, and today they were branding their Circle TB on the animals rumps. They had just finished with the last cow, when six Mexican pistoleros rode up.

"I am Capitan Francisco Guteraz, and these are my personal soldados," announced a swarthy looking man dressed in an old, faded uniform. "We have come to take possession of our cattle."

"Whadiya mean your cattle," exclaimed Gil Tripp.

"Did you not recently chase them out of the mesquite and cholla here?"

"Yeah, we did. So what?"

"Well, they are lost animals that have strayed from our herd."

"The hell you say!" replied Mike Barr. "They musta strayed some time ago 'cause they're all mossy back brush poppers that have been here for quite a spell. They was unbranded until we put our Circle TB on 'em."

"Ahh, yes. The branding. If I have some cattle and do not brand them, are they not still mine? What is a brand, Gringo? A man made mark on the hide. It means nothing to these cows that have Mexican souls."

"Mexican souls my ass. They're sure enough Texas Longhorns, and they're bunched on the American side of the Rio Grande!"

"They are but poor, dumb beasts that know nothing of political boundaries. They drink and swim in the river and step out wherever." The Capitan laughed.

"Well, how come you're just getting around to saving their souls now? How come you didn't bother with 'em before?" asked Tripp.

"They were very hard to find before." replied the Capitan. "Now that they are gathered, it is easier."

"So when you saw us rounding up these critters, you thought you would hop over and bluff us out of them. If you were really soldiers, you would know you have no authority on this side of the river. You're just a bunch of bandits."

"I go anywhere I please, Gringo. My soldados enforce my authority. We will take the cows now without trouble if you plan to live another day."

"Whadiya think, Gil?" asked Barr.

"I think maybe the Captain will die right here!"

The sixguns of the two Texas cowboys came out spitting a barrage of deadly lead. The over confident Capitan Guteraz took two slugs in the heart. Three soldados, shot off their horses, lay dead in the dusty desert. The other two Mexicans now sat slumped in the saddle. Shortly, they also would be dead.

Tripp and Barr had each taken a bullet. Gil in the thigh, and Mike in the upper arm. They bound up each other's injuries, and surveyed the grim scene.

"We was damn lucky, Mike. We could be sprawled here 'stead of them."

"True, but we sure couldn't just let 'em steal our cows. Aw, hell," sputtered Mike. "All that shootin' spooked 'em. If were lucky maybe we can find half."

Gil Tripp chuckled. "Well, at least we'll know which ones is ours. And maybe we can find some others with Mexican souls." ♣

COUNTER OFFER

The private railroad car parked at the siding of the Southern Pacific just outside Tucson, Arizona belonged to Jason Walker. He was president of the Arizona Stockman's Association, and one of the wealthiest land owners in the territory. Tonight he was entertaining Rachel Burlington in hopes her father, Hiram Burlington, owner of several business ventures in Tucson, would donate influence and money in behalf of Walkers bid for Governor.

The couple had just finished dinner, and were now sipping a fine Bordeaux, when three armed men burst into the coach. The young lady was too startled to move or utter a sound. Walker set his glass down on the table, and leaned back in his chair appearing quite at ease. "Would you gentlemen care for some wine?" he calmly asked.

"Well, aren't you the salty one," quipped the tall man in the middle. He stepped over to the table, picked up the wine bottle, and drank from it. Then he passed the bottle to his companions and remarked, "Not much kick, but tastes good."

"Now that we have all partaken in some refreshments," bantered Walker, "How may I help you?"

"You can open your safe and hand over all the cash you been collecting. Should be a might handsome amount, Governor."

"I'm not governor yet," chuckled Walker, "But I thank you for your vote of confidence. Also for your vote at the polls, I hope."

"Never mind all this palavering. Make him give us the money," snarled one of the other robbers.

"Please forgive such impetuousness, Mister Walker. Patience has never been one of his virtues," said the tall bandit. "However, he does have a point."

"And if I'm not inclined to cooperate?" intoned Walker.

"That could be fatal!" was the reply.

"Ah, but you won't get the money if you kill me. And you haven't got time to torture me," said Walker.

"But we could kill the young lady."

"No, you can only threaten to kill her. For if you were to actually kill her, you would lose **that threat**."

The tall robber scratched his chin and glared at Walker. "What the hell is goin' on here?" bellowed the third gunman.

Walker smiled. "Tell you what I'll do. I'll give each of you other fellows five hundred dollars if you shoot your tall friend."

The tall man took a couple of steps back and looked at his companions. He knew that they might do it.

Walker chuckled. "Maybe he'd like to earn the thousand for shooting the two of you."

The three robbers looked at each other with suspicion. Who could be trusted?

"Search him," said the tall robber. "We can split the thousand."

"Oh, I'm not carrying that much cash. It is available here in this coach. But to search for it takes time. And time is running out." Walker continued in his nonchalant manner. "The young lady will be expected home. If she doesn't return soon, her father will suspect that something is wrong and send some men."

The three robbers stared at Walker. He could see that they were uncertain as to what to do. "Now come on, boys," he drawled. "Either someone start shooting or clear out."

The tall man cocked his single action Colt. Watching his companions carefully, he backed out of the railroad coach. His bewildered partners quickly followed him.

Walker stood, walked to the doorway, and leaned out. "Don't forget to vote." ♣

THE SEAL

Rose Kelly's body was found Saturday morning in the oak grove near the barn where the dance had been held Friday night. There were bruises on her face, and her neck was broken. Although her blouse and skirt were both torn, it didn't appear that she had been sexually assaulted.

"I guess that's something to be thankful for," her mother said in a trance. But that didn't relieve the suffering of the grieving parents.

Father Murphy, the local priest, offered consolation and prayer, as did all the citizens of Douglas. Sunday service was dedicated to Rose and her family. The congregation was devastated that this lovely young girl's life had been so brutally taken.

Sheriff Charley Bates vowed to find the killer. During the next few day he questioned everyone who had attended the dance.

Late Monday evening Father Murphy was hearing confessions. "Bless me, Father, for I have sinned," began the young man. Then only the heavy breathing of the penitent could be heard.

"Take your time," said Father Murphy. "How can I help you?"

"Father, I ... I ..." stammered the man. "I killed Rose Kelly," he blurted.

The priest was stunned for a moment. He tried to remain calm, and spoke in a quiet voice. "Tell me about it, son."

"I didn't mean to kill her. At first all I wanted was a kiss, but when she struggled, I got upset. I tore her blouse, and pushed her down. That's when her skirt ripped open, and she started to holler. I grabbed her by the hair, and hit her a couple of times just to make her keep quiet. And then she just laid there with her head twisted funny. I got scared and ran." The young man started to cry. "I didn't mean to kill her, Father. I didn't mean ..." his voice drifted off.

"This is a very grievous sin," said the priest, "but God forgives all who are truly sorry."

"Oh, lord. Oh, yes! I am sorry, Father. I truly wish it had never happened."

"God forgives you, son. Make a good act of contrition. For your penance I want you to pray in church every day for the next month. Now go in peace."

Father Murphy sat in the confessional waiting for the next penitent. None came. The burden of this last confession was heavy. The priest prayed that God would help him to bear this cross.

By the end of the week Sheriff Bates had finished his investigation, and had arrested Johnny Dawson. This young man had been seen walking with Rose out to the oak grove. A search had revealed a bracelet that belonged to Rose was in his pants pocket.

Dawson admitted being in the oak grove with Rose. But he swore he hadn't harmed her in any way. She was alive when he left the oak grove. She wanted to stay there for awhile and look at the stars. She gave him the bracelet as a token of affection. "I didn't kill her!" he pleaded.

Sheriff Bates held Dawson in custody at the jail. He admitted that the evidence was circumstantial, but there didn't seem to be any other suspects, and the Douglas citizens were outraged and demanded justice.

Father Murphy visited Johnny Dawson in his cell. They talked for a while. The young man insisted he was innocent. The priest tried to comfort him, expressing belief in his story.

As Father Murphy passed through the sheriff's office, Bates asked, "So, what do you think, Father?"

"He didn't do it," was the priest's reply.

"And what makes you believe that?" asked Bates.

"I'm just certain he didn't kill Rose. I can't give you any proof."

"God has given you some insight. Is that it?" remarked Bates.

"Something like that," replied the priest as he left the jail.

For the next couple of weeks Father Murphy was a troubled man. Dawson's voice was completely different from that of the young man who had confessed to killing Rose. The priest knew that Johnny Dawson was innocent. But the "Seal of Confessional" prevented him disclosing any knowledge.

Dawson's trial was brief. The prosecuting attorney presented the evidence that was the basis for believing Johnny Dawson had killed Rose Kelly. The defense stressed that all that was purely circumstantial. That no one had actually seen the killing. However, the jury was more influenced by the emotions of the town, than by rational consideration. Johnny Dawson was found guilty, and sentenced to hang.

Father Murphy was tormented by both his knowledge and his sense of helplessness. The hanging was scheduled in a few days.

Father Murphy entered the church and saw a young man kneeling there. The priest knelt down beside him. "Do you mind if I join you in prayer?" The young man looked at the priest, then bowed his head, but said nothing. Father Murphy's voice was soft, but could be heard by the young man. "I pray that who-ever killed Rose Kelly will turn himself into Sheriff Bates. It would be terrible, if for the rest of his life, his conscience had to bear the responsibility for two deaths." The priest then left the church.

Jeff Chapman rode out of Douglas that night, and was never seen again.

The next morning, miraculously, a note would be found pushed under the door of the sheriff's office.

I Killed Rose Kelly!

Jeff Chapman

Father Murphy's prayers would be answered.

Alas, no miracle occurred. Father Murphy wept when Johnny Dawson was hanged. ♣

CUES

Abel Shank dressed all in black pushed through the batwing doors of the Silver Palace, paused to look around, and then crossed to a table at the rear of the saloon.

"Billy McCoy, you cagey wolf," he said.

"I was sparked ta git yer wire. Heard you was grim."

"That was whiskers ta get the chrushers off me back," replied McCoy laughing.

"That was fly," chuckled Shank.

"Glad ta set me glimmers on ya, Abel."

"Same here," smiled Shank. "Snapped ta cap yer lay."

"Plummy. I got a mark. He's dusty. So I need a oak cousin."

"He flush?" asked Shank.

"Rhino fat. Dead game!"

"So, patter the flash."

"He's a black-spy cattle buyer. Keeps his skep in the bank 'til he needs it."

"So, we tob him, hoist and speel?"

"No, I got a better play with a bigger bag. This is the deal." McCoy explained the set-up.

A few days latter the cattle buyer, Sam Mason, was stopped by McCoy and Shank.

"I haven't much money," he said. "You gentlemen are wasting your time."

"Ah, but yer on ta the bank ta get some, and we're goin' with ya. Don't try peachin' ta the tappers. Me rusty cull has a quick shiv," hissed McCoy.

Mason starred at them in silence.

"When we git ta the bank, yer gonna draw out a hunnerd thousand bucks. If any noddle act smokey about us, you say we'er with ya ta protect such a large pony. You sharp with that?"

"Your idiom is somewhat enigmatic," said Mason, "but I get the general idea."

McCoy squinted and snarled, "Well, you best be stone square, er else!"

The three men entered the bank, and Mason walked to the desk of the assistant manager.

"Good morning, Ellis."

"Good morning, Mister Mason. Are you making a withdrawal again to buy more cattle?"

Mason remained calm and smiling replied, "A bit more than usual today. One hundred thousand dollars. These men are acting as body guards." Reaching for a pen he said, "I injured my hand last night. Ellis, would you mind filling out the withdrawal form for me to sign. I'll need the money in cash,"

Ellis paused for just a moment and replied, "I will be happy to assist, Sir. For such a large amount of cash I will have to arrange everything with Mister Baker." Ellis crossed to the bank president's office and entered. He returned in a couple of minutes and said, "Everything is prepared." He filled out the form and handed it to Mason, who, with a flourish, scrawled a signature.

Then Ellis said, "For security of such a large withdrawal Mister Baker has asked that the money be transferred to you in his office. If you gentlemen would please follow me."

Ellis held open the door to Baker's office and the three men entered. McCoy and Shank were immediately apprehended by four policemen.

"What the bloody hell?" yelled McCoy. "Shit!... What tumbled us?"

Ellis smiled. "When Mister Mason reached for the pen, he took it in his right hand. Mister Mason is left handed." ♣

WAKAN-TANKA

S eth Carr moved cautiously through the brush lined arroyo, keeping close to the high banks when possible. He had lost his horse a few miles back when he was jumped by three Comanche braves. They would have killed him for sure if they had waited a bit more, but one of them got antsy and attacked too soon.

When his horse went down, Seth took cover behind the dead animal in time to shoot two of the charging Indians. Then he rolled away and managed to scramble into some nearby rocks.

Seth's buckskin shirt and faded denims blended well into the desert landscape. This allowed him to slip away from the ambush site. But the third Comanche was still on his trail.

This third warrior was a patient, steady stalker. Riding his pony sometimes, but more often leading his mount. The Indian was being careful also, lest he fall to the white man's gun.

The Comanche had one advantage. He had water. Seth's canteen was still on his dead horse. Seth's destination was then mandated by this simple fact. It had rained several times during the last couple of weeks. Rio San Pedro should be running wet. The Comanche might guess that was where Seth was going, and get ahead of him and wait. If he was going to survive, Seth would need a great deal of skill and stealth, combined with a hell of a lot of luck.

Raven followed the white man's trail long enough to determine where it was leading. He was sure now that his enemy was headed for Rio San Pedro. Raven mounted his pony, and raced to get there first, to find a place to wait and watch.

Seth was getting close to the San Pedro. He moved even more slowly and carefully now, suspecting that the Comanche was there waiting for him. He paused beside a Mesquite tree, and glancing down, was attracted by a bright shining object on the ground. He knelt to examine it.

Raven saw the white man stop just short of the bank of the Rio San Pedro. It was an easy shot. Raven drew his bow and released the arrow. Just as the arrow left the bow, the white man knelt.

The arrow quivered in the tree near Seth, just a couple of inches above his back. He flattened to ground, and rolled a few feet away. Then springing to his feet, he raced through the brush and Mesquite trees. He abandoned stealth for speed at the moment.

Raven muttered a Comanche oath as he saw the arrow fly above the kneeling white man. He ran to where his enemy had knelt. Raven looked down. There on the ground lay a sparkling broken Indian bracelet. This worthless wrist band had saved the white man's life.

After some distance Seth stopped to listen. He didn't hear or see the Comanche, but then that was also true, when the arrow had barely missed.

Seth needed water so he took a chance and stepped out of the brush long enough to get a drink Returning into the brush, Seth followed the San Pedro. Then nearby he heard some voices. Moving very slowly, he eased through the brush until he could see who was there.

Two very rough looking men wearing ponchos were sitting, sharing whiskey from a bottle. Seth noticed a bound and gagged Indian girl laying across from them.

"Scalp hunters," muttered Seth to himself. Renegades who traded Indian scalps to the Mexicans for gold. And often traded captive Indian girls as well.

Seth stepped into the small clearing where the men sat. Pointing his rifle at them he said coldly, "Don't make a move!" Crossing to the captive girl, Seth drew his knife and cut the rope binding her feet. He motioned for her to stand.

Still keeping his rifle trained on the two scalp hunters, Seth cut the rope that tied her hands. The girl removed the gag from her mouth but said nothing.

Seth gestured for the girl to run away, but she stood still. As he started to back out of the clearing, she moved with him.

"I probably should shoot scum like you," said Seth. "Don't reckon I know why I don't. Guess it's just your lucky day." Seth and the Indian girl melted into the brush.

Raven had heard the scalp hunters talking about the same time Seth had. He had seen Seth free the girl. He decided this was why Wakan-Tanka had saved the white man's life with the broken bracelet. To free this Indian girl.

And the Great Spirit had also guided the white man's hand not to kill the scalp hunters. Now Raven could have this honor. The arrows from his bow pierced the chest of each of them. Then he hurried after his enemy.

Raven caught up with the white man and the Indian girl a short time later. The white man didn't see him, but the girl did. Just as he was about to release an arrow, the girl stepped between. Why was Wakan-Tanka protecting this white man now?

Just then a large tawny cat leaped from the rocks above Raven. The white man's rifle thundered, and the mountain lion lay dead at Raven's feet.

The Indian girl smiled at Seth. Then she crossed over to Raven and took his hand. Seth nodded to the pair, and walked away. Raven decided The Great Spirit was very wise. ♣

HORSE TRADE

Trace Bedlow was an Arizona mustang runner. His daddy had been a mule skinner and bronc breaker, and had taught Trace such skills. Trace never had much formal schooling, but he sure knew horses.

Trace wasn't a big man. Only five foot nine and one hundred sixty five pounds. But he was all muscle, with quick hands and agile feet. His skill with a rope was unparalleled, and his ability to ease up on a herd of mustangs was incredible.

Trace had a contract to provide horses for the Army at Fort Lowell, which was just outside Tucson. He had gathered and partly broke fifteen mustangs that he was delivering today. They were all mares, 14 or 15 hands high. Bays and sorrels, just what the U.S Cavalry wanted. Since they were only partly broke, he put a hackamore on each one, and attached a lead rope so they would trail better.

Watching a hawk gliding high with the wind, and musing about what he might do in Tucson after being paid, he was startled by two gunshots.

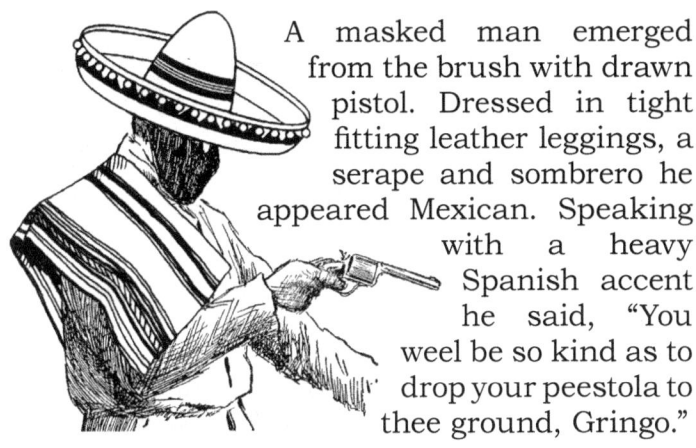

A masked man emerged from the brush with drawn pistol. Dressed in tight fitting leather leggings, a serape and sombrero he appeared Mexican. Speaking with a heavy Spanish accent he said, "You weel be so kind as to drop your peestola to thee ground, Gringo."

Trace carefully eased his colt from its holster and dropped it.

"Now you weel pleese dismount," was the next command. Trace complied.

"Ahh, for these veriee fine horses I thank you. You must walk only a mile, maybe, to find your saddled aneemal that I leeve for you. Adios."

Trace watched disgustedly as the bandit rode off with his mustangs. He started walking and was surprised and thankful to find his saddle horse as promised.

Riding into Tucson, Trace was stunned as he passed Rafe McQueen's livery. There in the confines of the attached corral were his fifteen mustang mares. The hackamores hadn't even been removed.

As Trace dismounted, Rafe McQueen stepped from the building. "Afternoon, Trace. How ya doin'?"

Trace smiled and replied, "I wasn't doin' so well a while ago, when my string a mustangs string got stole, but now I see you recovered 'em for me."

"I don't reckon I follow yer drift," said McQueen with a smirk.

"Them mustangs," said Trace pointing. "They're the ones I was deliverin' ta Fort Lowell before they was stole."

"You ain't sayin' I stole yer horses, are ya?" snarled McQueen.

"I ain't supposin' how they come ta be in yer corral. I'm only statin' the fact that they're the mustangs I gathered and partly broke. They still got the hackamores I put on 'em."

McQueen folded his arms across his chest and replied, "I don't see how you can be so almighty sure a that, Trace, seein' as how they ain't branded. And I don't know nobody who can tell one rope hackamore from another, so they don't prove nothin'."

"I was supposed to deliver them to the Army today," stammered Trace.

"I see," said McQueen. "Well, maybe ya still can. I'll sell 'em to ya."

"You 'spect me ta pay you for my own horses!" fumed Trace.

"I was just thinkin', if ya want ta deliver horses ta the Army today, ya might want ta buy the ones I got. 'Course, if ya cant fill the contract ya got, maybe the Army might buy from me. But I don't want ta cause you ta lose that contract."

"Why you miserable, connivin' skunk," shouted Trace. Rafe McQueen only laughed.

"I'll make ya a deal," said McQueen. "I understand the Army is paying fifty dollars a head. I'll sell fer twenty five, and you can still make some profit."

Trace scowled in silence. Then he said, "I ain't got that much money on me."

"The bank's still open," retorted McQueen.

Grumbling Trace mounted and rode to the Tucson Bank. He came back and grudgingly gave McQueen $375.00. McQueen laughed as Trace headed for Fort Lowell with his mustangs.

That night a man dressed as a Mexican broke into McQueen's sleeping quarters and robbed him at gunpoint of $375.00.

When Rafe McQueen confronted Trace about this incident, Trace shrugged and suggested, "Musta been that same Mexican that stole my mustangs." ♣

TEACHER

Alfred Mason sat relaxed as the stagecoach bounced across the Arizona desert. He was a slender man just under five foot ten with a humorously oafish face. Spectacles, wire rimmed, perched on a round nose enabling him to focus hound dog eyes on a newspaper held by big bony hands.

Reading the title, "Tombstone Epitaph", he smiled, for he was nearing the end of his journey which had started in Saint Louis, Missouri. This last leg by stagecoach from Benson would take him to Tombstone where he was to assume the duties of school teacher.

As the stage rolled to a stop in front of the recently opened "Grand Hotel", Alfred waited patiently for the other passengers to exit. He then stepped into the dust of Tombstone's Allen Street.

Brute Jenkins stood among the throng of townsfolk gathered for the arrival of the bi- weekly stage from Benson. He had been christened Brutus at birth, and the name was prophetic for he had become an ugly ill-tempered brute bully. Brute's attention immediately centered on the spectacled, meek looking man holding a small satchel.

Alfred Mason removed his eye glasses and slipped them into an inside coat pocket. Blinking in the bright sunlight he gawked at the busy western town. Glancing up the street, he started toward Nellie Cashman's Arcade Restaurant and Chop House.

Brute stepped in front of Alfred, snarling, "Well now, Clown. What be your name?"

Caught by surprise, Alfred retreated a couple of steps and stammered, "Uh. Uh." He started to say Alfred, but only got out Al before Brute shouted, "Alice . This clowns name is Alice. Now ain't he cute?"

Astonished by this sudden confrontation, Alfred stood speechless gaping at the bully.

Brute reached out and grabbed hold of the satchel in Alfred's hand, "Whatcha got in the bag, Alice?"

Saying nothing, Alfred firmly pulled the satchel from Brute's fingers.

Brute reached for the satchel again and growled, "I said whatcha got in the bag?" Jerking the satchel from Alfred's hand, Brute snapped, "Why don't I just have a looksee?"

Alfred starred at Brute and calmly said, "Please put the satchel down, Sir."

"Sir!" roared Brute. "He called me, Sir, and said please. Now, ain't he the polite one." Glaring at Alfred he snarled, "Just what kind of dandy are you, Alice?"

"I'm a teacher," replied Mason evenly. "And my name is Alfred."

"Well, as far as I can tell, Alice is more fitting," smirked Brute. "Now let's see what's in this bag."

Alfred gently touched Brute's hand and simply said, "No."

"No?" screamed Brute. "You really think ya can stop me, Alice? I'll squash ya like a little bug. You'll be beggin' me ta look in yer crummy bag!"

"I do not wish to brawl with you, Sir. However, as a teacher, I feel obligated to provide you with an appropriate lesson."

Two straight, hard, rocking left jabs struck Brute squarely in the jaw. They were quickly followed by an equally jarring right to the solar plexus. Before Brute could recover from the shock of these sudden explosive fists, two more straight, solid left jabs broke Brute's nose. Then a hammering right cross to the head dropped Brute into the dust of Allen Street.

Looking down at the nearly unconscious bully sprawled in the dust, Alfred Mason calmly said, "I trust that I have taught you to have proper respect for your fellow man. You may also consider this as a lesson in humility, and should teach you to never under estimate an opponent."♣

THE NOVICE

As young Tom Olsen rode into Bisbee, two men were dismounting in front of the mercantile. "That's a mighty pretty Indian pony ya got there, son," said one of them.

"Thanks," replied the boy. "I'm mighty proud of Patches." Tom was a fifteen year old lad with sandy colored hair, and freckles.

"How'd ya like ta make an easy dollar?" asked the man.

"Well, I can always use a dollar. What do I have ta do?"

"My friend and I need to buy some goods in the mercantile. Our horses are skitterish, and don't like to be tied. You just sit here on your pony and hold their reins. Here's a dollar."

The lad took the reins and the dollar, and sat there on his pony while the two men went into the mercantile.

The two men returned in a few minutes carrying some supplies which they put in there saddlebags. "Thanks, son. Now we have some business just across the street. Here's another dollar," said the man smiling. The boy smiled back, and nodded.

This time when the two men came back they were running. They leaped onto their horses, and one hollered, "You'd best jump start that pony quick and ride, 'cause we just robbed the bank."

Tom Olsen was startled. He heard a gun shot, and Patches bolted after the other two horses. The next thing he knew, he was galloping out of Bisbee along side of two bank robbers.

A while later, figuring it was safe to stop, the bank robbers reined up in a wash that was lined with mesquite trees. "We should be in the clear now. They couldn't get up a posse quick enough ta catch us. Ya did real good, son. What's yer name?"

"Tom Olsen," replied the boy.

"Well, Tom, yer a first class bank robber now. Yessiree."

"I ain't no bank robber," stammered Tom. "You tricked me, and I rode after you 'cause they was shootin', and Patches bolted."

"Maybe the folks back in Bisbee won't see it that way, what with you holdin' the horses for us. And that paint Indian pony yer ridin' is right easy ta spot. My name is Chad Thorn and he's Brad Bennet."

"But I don't want ta be a outlaw."

"You ain't got much choice right at the moment. We don't aim ta let ya leave us fer awhile. Specially since I just give ya our names. And we may need ya ta hold our horses again"

"I won't tell anyone yer names if ya let me ride away."

"Well, we'll think on it. Meantime you'd best ride along with us. Safer that way fer you and us."

When they made camp that night, Chad said, "Tom, we could tie ya up ta keep ya here. We won't do that if ya give us yer word that ya won't run off. It'd be uncomfortable fer ya ta sleep tied up." Tom looked at the two men in silence.

"Keep in mind what I told ya about yer pony bein' easy ta spot. If ya run, we'll find ya, and we won't be so gentle then."

"Ok, I understand, said Tom. "Where do you want me to sleep?"

And so Tom stayed with Chad and Brad for the next week. It worried him that he was riding the outlaw trail, but he didn't see any way ta change that at present. At least the two robbers were jovial company and treated him ok.

The trio rode into Douglas. Tom was told to hold the horses just as he had done in Bisbee.

"Don't try anything clever, son," warned Chad. "One of us is sure ta find ya. Brad'll be watchin' ya from just inside the bank."

As the outlaws burst out of the bank two shots were fired from within. One bullet struck Chad in the leg. With Brad's help he mounted his horse, and the three men raced out of Douglas.

Hidden in an old abandoned barn, Chad examined his leg. The wound was not fatal. The bullet had gone through without breaking bone. But it was painful, and using the leg was difficult.

"Now are you gonna let me go?" asked Tom.

"Sorry, son, but now we need ya more than ever. Yer gonna hafta go into the bank with Brad on the next job, while I hold the horses," said Chad.

"I can't do that," pleaded Tom. "I don't know what ta do. I sure ain't gonna shoot anybody."

"Ya won't hafta shoot. Yer gun won't even be loaded. But them people in the bank won't know that. You just follow Brad and make it look like yer his backup."

"Can't we wait 'til yer leg is healed?"

"No we can't. The bank in Tombstone is loaded right now. We gotta hit it before they transfer the money ta someplace else."

It was a quiet Thursday morning when they reined their horses in front of the Tombstone Bank. *Oh Lord, how do I get outta this mess?* thought Tom.

It wasn't until he was inside the bank that Tom had an inspiration. Since being with the outlaws, this was the first time that Brad and Chad had been separated. Chad was outside, and Tom was behind Brad. Tom's gun was empty, but it was a big, heavy Walker and still made a good club. Tom walked over and struck Brad in the back of the head with the gun. The outlaw dropped to the floor unconscious.

"Tie this man up quick," said Tom. Then he turned and stepped into the street where Chad was waiting. As Tom walked up to the horses, Chad bellowed, "Where the hell is Brad?"

"He ain't comin'," replied Tom as he swung the empty Walker, striking Chad in the knee of his injured leg. The outlaw shrieked in pain. Tom brought the heavy gun down on the injured leg a second time, and as Chad doubled over his knee in agony, Tom slugged him behind the ear with the Walker. Chad slid off his horse and lay in the dust of Allen Street.

"I never wanted ta be a outlaw," explained Tom as he sat in the office of Marshall Billy Breakenridge. ♣

APPLES AND SUGAR

Emmet Grant sat in a rocking chair by the fireplace puffing on his pipe. It was Wednesday, and Emmet was enjoying a relaxing afternoon. Normally he would be working at the Bedford Mercantile which he owned. But his wife, Martha, had finally convinced him to take a day off. So Emmet reluctantly let his clerk, Bud Farley, manage the store for the day.

Martha was busy in the kitchen when Emmet heard her say, "Oh, for lands sake."

"What's the matter, Honey?" he called.

"Well, I was going to bake you an apple pie, but I discovered I haven't got enough apples or sugar."

Emmet rose quickly. "Why then, I'll just go into the store and get some." The Grant home was only about a mile from the town business district.

"Now you just sit and relax," responded Martha. "This is supposed to be your day away from the store."

"I'm not goin' in ta work, Martha. I sure would like that pie."

"Oh, you're just using that as an excuse to check on Bud."

"No, I'm not. I have complete confidence in Bud. I won't bother him at all. I'll just pop in long enough ta get the apples and sugar." So Emmet hitched up his horse and buggy and drove into Bedford.

True to his word to Martha, Emmet didn't linger in the store. Bud was busy with some other customers, so Emmet helped himself to some sugar and a bag of apples, and exited the Mercantile.

As he was putting the groceries into his buggy, Emmet heard a shriek. He turned and saw a man strike a woman and shake her roughly. Emmet walked over to the couple and said, "That's no way to treat a lady, Sir."

"Mind yer own business, Jackass," slurred the ruffian.

"You've been drinking, Sir," replied Emmet. "I'm sure if you were sober you wouldn't mistreat a woman."

"Butt out, you little pipsqueak, before I bash you into pulp." The drunk swung a fist at Emmet, who easily dodged the wild punch. Enraged the ruffian lunged violently at Emmet, who dodged again. But this time he tripped his assailant, who crashed head- long into the side of a nearby building. The ruffian lay on the boardwalk unconscious. Emmet tipped his hat to the woman, smiled, and walked away.

Emmet decided that after this encounter he could use a drink himself. Stepping through the batwing doors of the Longhorn Saloon, he crossed to the bar and ordered a beer. As he sipped his beer his attention was drawn to a very loud argument, which resulted in gunplay. A local cowboy lay on the floor, while a stranger stood holding his Colt.

"You saw it," shouted the stranger. "He drew first. You all saw it."

Through some murmuring and nodding, Emmet spoke. "You drew first."

The gunman turned toward Emmet. "You callin' me a liar?"

"Oh, no, Sir," said Emmet smiling. "But you said we all saw it. So, I'm just stating what I saw."

The gunman blinked and scowled, as Emmet continued. "You was movin' yer right hand and wigglin' them fingers, and that other fella was watchin' that, just like most of the men in this room. But your left gun had already cleared leather, when the other fella reached for his gun."

"Yer a liar!" snarled the gunman.

"I'm just sayin' what I saw," replied Emmet.

"I said yer a liar. What're gonna do about it?"

"Nothing," said Emmet calmly as he turned his back and ordered another beer.

The gunman stood dumbfounded and speechless. By now some of the other men were holding guns, so the stranger backed out of the saloon and rode out of Bedford.

Several men now crowded around Emmet. "That was damned nervy, Fella." one of them remarked. "And you, not even wearin' a gun." Emmet shrugged, finished his beer, walked out.

As Emmet was returning to his buggy, a couple of gunshots were heard coming from the Bedford Bank. Two men holding money bags rushed out, jumped on their horses, and charged down the street.

Emmet ran to his buggy, and grabbed his lever action Winchester from the boot. The two bank robbers were galloping toward him shooting.

With bullets wizzing past, Emmet calmly stood and raised the Winchester. He fired twice, knocking both bank robbers from their horses. As Bedford's sheriff and some of the men from the saloon gathered up the wounded bank robbers, Emmet returned his Winchester to the boot, climbed into the buggy, and drove home.

Martha was standing on the front porch waiting for him. "You were gone longer than expected," she said. "I was worried you might have got in trouble."

Emmet grinned and drawled, "Awh, Honey. How much trouble could I get into just goin' ta get apples and sugar?" ♣

CROOKED FOOT

With the Comanches terrorizing settlers along the Rio Grande on both sides of the border, and threatening the safety of travelers following El Camino Real de Tierra Adentro, the major trade route between Mexico City and San Juan Pueblo, New Mexico, the 2nd U.S. Dragoons, under the command of Major Marshall Howell, was sent to Fort Conrad.

Luke Chambers was scouting for a troop from Fort Conrad in pursuit of a band of Comanches

being led by a warrior named Crooked Foot. Luke had only seen Crooked Foot once, some twenty years ago. At that time the warrior was only five years old. Luke found him caught in a mountain lion trap, his ankle broken and twisted. Luke had released the boy from the trap, and carried him several miles before leaving him just outside a Comanche camp. The boy could crawl from there and call for help. It was ironic that the young Indian he had saved was now the scourge of Texas and New Mexico.

The troop had stopped to rest in a dry wash. Dismounted, they were seeking relief from the scorching sun by sitting in the shade of the Mesquite trees on both sides of the wash, when the Comanches attacked.

The ambush was well executed and a complete surprise. The Dragoons had chased Crooked Foot until his warriors had caught the troopers. It was now every man for himself in hopes of surviving.

Luke jumped up on the bank of the wash, shooting two Comanches on the way. He figured it was better to fight in the brush filled desert, than be trapped in the wash. He hoped some of the troopers had made the same decision. Maybe a couple of them could have mounted and escaped, but very few would have had the time.

Luke eased cautiously through the brush, moving away from the wash. He was forced to shoot another brave. He wasn't too happy about that, since the shot would reveal his location.

Luke had run a short distance in order to change positions, and had managed to get a couple hundred yards from the wash, when he came face to face with three Comanches. One of them was Crooked Foot.

Crooked Foot looked at his companions and made a sign not to shoot. "Well, Old Man. It has been many moons."

"That it has," replied Luke.

"You saved me then. I not forget that. I bear the memory every time I walk. Now you lead the pony soldiers to capture or kill me."

"You are no longer a helpless little boy," answered Luke.

Crooked Foot nodded. "You should have killed me when you had the chance. You would have saved a great many lives." Luke shrugged and remained silent.

"Do you think I should spare you now in return?" asked Crooked Foot. Again Luke shrugged.

"I cannot do that. You are an enemy. My warriors would not understand." Luke listened and waited. Crooked Foot had something in mind.

"I will kill you, Old Man. But it will be a fair fight. You have a knife. Is it a good knife?"

"Yes, it is," replied Luke drawing his heavy Bowie knife.

Crooked Foot removed his own knife from the sheath at his waist, and went into a fighting crouch.

Luke knew he was in trouble. The Comanche was younger, stronger, and quicker. And probably more practiced in knife fighting. Still, at least there was some chance, even if it was slim.

Luke watched as Crooked Foot flashed the knife from hand to hand, and then lashed out. Luke did not try to counter with his own knife. He dodged away instead. Watch for an opportunity he thought. Twice more the Comanche thrust, and twice more Luke dodged.

Luke shifted the way he was holding the handle of the knife. This time as Crooked Foot lunged, Luke stepped toward him, and hurled the heavy Bowie knife with all his strength. The distance was only a few feet, and the sharp, heavy blade penetrated the Comanche's chest, buried to the hilt.

Crooked Foot gasped, sunk to his knees, and pitched forward. Luke rushed to the fallen Comanche, and scooped up Crooked Foot's knife. He followed by charging the two remaining Comanches, who seemed to be paralyzed in shock at the death of their leader. Luke crashed into the closest warrior, knocking him into the other brave, who fell. Crooked Foot's knife sunk deep into the standing Comanche. Then Luke leaped on the fallen brave. They struggled for possession of the Indian's rifle. Luke managed to get the barrel pointed at the Comanche, and pull the trigger.

Luke stood holding the rifle, watching for more Comanches. None came.

Walking over to where Crooked Foot lay, Luke looked down. "I reckon Fate figured the life I saved was mine to take." ♣

THE BOOK

"Far off, three mountain tops, three pinnacles of aged snow, stood sunset-flushed." Jonas Simon spoke with quiet reverence as his eyes peered at the pages of the book he was holding. Abel Davis, Tobias Meeker and Hiram Barnes listened intently as Jonas narrated from his book. This was a Saturday night ritual at the Restful Hollow Nursing Home.

Jonas continued, "And dewed with showery drops, up-clomb the shadowy pine above the woven copse." Jonas sighed and turned a page.

The book was leather bound. Black. Gilded on the cover with a gold fleur-de-lis. Abel Davis thought the book was magnificent. The poetry and stories that filled his senses each Saturday night were beyond wonderful.

Abel had asked Jonas to let him borrow the book. Although the refusal had been politely calm, Abel was not content.

Jonas was speaking again, another poem. Abel was dreaming of possessing the book for himself. His mind now refocused on this new narration.

"The rainbows that we chase we need not find to hold the pot of gold within our mind." Jonas paused. His eyes shifted to the next page. "For stardust that glimmers, and moon beams that shimmer, we are never too old. So dream on with passion, the visions we fashion are precious as gold." Jonas smiled and closed the book.

Abel was enthralled by the words. His dream of possessing the book was intensified. He coveted the book.

For the next few weeks Abel's longing for the book was an obsession. He must have it. Day an night he was haunted by the thought of having the book for his very own. As the Saturday night sessions continued, they were no longer satisfying to Abel. Once, when Jonas closed the book at the end of the evening, and it lay on his lap, Abel touched the cover with his palm. A thrilling spasm shot through Abel, and a feeling of euphoria coarsed his entire body.

When Jonas suddenly came down with the flu, Abel became excited. If Jonas were to die, Abel could steal the book, and say it was given to him. The obsession became an evil desire.

It was near midnight when Abel slipped quietly into the bedroom where Jonas was sleeping. He glanced about the room and saw the book on the dresser next to the bed. For an instant it seemed like his heart had stopped beating, and his head was swimming. Abel moved slowly and silently to the edge of the bed. Since Jonas was already breathing irregularly from the flu, it took little effort to smother him with a pillow. Abel took the book and hurried back to his own room.

Abel sat clutching the book. He held it to his chest in a loving embrace. He laid the book in his lap and gazed at it enraptured. He carefully opened the beautiful cover and began turning pages.

An agonizing scream exploded from Abel's throat, and then he began to sob. All the pages in the book were blank. ♣

Soar with the Wandering Winds.
Let them sing through the canyons
Of your imagination

ALSO BY JAMES J. HUBLE

APPEARANCES

A Collection of
16 Western Short Stories
ISBN# 978-0-9825963-7-1

TWISTED TRAILS

A Collection of
18 Western Short Stories
each with a 'Twist'
ISBN# 978-1-939345-04-2

TANGLED TAPESTRY

A Collection of
19 Western Short Stories
ISBN# 978-1-939345-07-3

Available from
Goose Flats Publishing
P.O. Box 813
Tombstone, Arizona, 85638
www.gooseflats.com

Amazon.com

BarnesAndNoble.com

and from the Author.

Dealer inquiries welcomed

ABOUT THE AUTHOR

James Huble is retired and lives in the Catalina foothills north of Tucson Arizona. He taught English, speech, dramatics, and philosophy; is a published poet and a song writer, and has performed professionally as a musician and actor. When writing these  short stories, you might say he assumed the role of a chuck wagon cook; rustling up a pot full of situations, stirring in a little theatrical flavor, and seasoning with a mischievous perspective.

CPSIA information can be obtained
at www.ICGtesting.com
Printed in the USA
FSHW01n2337070718
49992FS

9 781939 345196